I'm a Princess Hairdresser

Royal Hair Salon

What a busy morning at the Royal Hair Salon! The hairdryers are whirring, shampoo is bubbling and everyone's singing along to the music. Combs, curlers and conditioner are at the ready. And look, your first customer is Princess Ruby!

Twinkle Toes

Turn to the last page to choose a lovely new hairstyle for Princess Ruby!

Princess Ruby has lots of favourite things she loves to do. One of them is going to Isabelle's ice cream parlour. Her best friends always meet her there to taste strawberry sundaes, chocolate chip cookie specials and rainbow milkshakes. Yummy-scrummy!

Turn to the last page and pick a treat-time hairstyle for Ruby!

In the summer, Princess Ruby likes having a picnic with all her friends and their fun and fluffy pets. There are kittens to cuddle, ponies to pet and puppies to tickle. The sun glows in the sky, butterflies flutter and little birds chirp happily.

Turn to the last page and pick a picnic-perfect hairstyle for Ruby!

Winter Funtime

When winter comes and snowflakes start to sprinkle, Princess Ruby and her friends love to slide on their ice skates. Round and round they twirl, circling and gliding, dancing on ice. What a magical time with twinkling fairy lights and laughter everywhere!

Turn to the last page and choose a wonderful winter look for Ruby.

Princess Party

Princess Party

But best of all, Princess Ruby loves a party! With a swish of silk and a swoosh of satin, Ruby's friends arrive in their finest frocks. Everyone's ready to dance the night away and play princess party games, and of course... giggle, giggle, giggle!

Princess Party

Turn to the last page and select a brilliant party-look for Ruby!

Princess Hairstyles

Choose from these hairstyles for Ruby as you go through the pages.

Perfect ponytail

1 Turn Ruby so that you see the back of her head.

2 Pull all the hair through the band. The ponytail is ready!

Use your comb first to make the hair smooth.

Brilliant bunches

1 Divide the hair into two sections of the same size.

2 Tie the section on the left with a band.

3 Tie the section on the right with a band. Such pretty bunches!

Half hair ponytail

1 Move two small sections of hair to the front.

2 Join the two sections at the back.

3 Tie the mini ponytail together with a band.